SESAME STREET

W9-CEQ-337

Rise and Shine!

By Constance Allen
Cover Illustrated by Joe Ewers
Illustrated by David Prebenna

Printed in the U.S.A.
ISBN: 1-40373-233-7 (X)

07 08 09 10 BM 10 9 8 7 6 5 4 3 2 1
15424 Sesame Street 8x8 Storybook: Rise and Shine

123
SESAME STREET
Rise and Shine!

DO NOT
DISTURB

Rise and shine! The sun is coming up! On Sesame Street, little monsters and birds and grouches are still snug in their beds.

Barkley is ready for an early morning walk.
The baker is baking cookies and cakes and bread.
Up and at 'em, everyone—or there won't be any left!

Ernie wakes up his buddy Bert.
"Rise and shine, Bert! The sun is coming up!"

Time to get up, Mommy and Daddy! Baby Natasha is ready to play!

In the country, Farmer Grover gets ready to milk the cows.
"Rise and shine, little cows!" he calls.

In the city, Oscar wakes up to watch the trash collectors. “Bang those cans!” he yells. “That’s it, boys! Crash ’em! Clank ’em! Heh-heh-heh.”

The Count is up early, delivering newspapers.
"One newspaper! Two newspapers! Three newspapers!"
he counts. "Rise and shine, everyone!
It's a marvelous day for counting!"

“Rise and shine!” calls Sherry Netherland. It’s time for Benny the bellhop to get to work.

Herry Monster huffs and puffs on his morning jog.

"What should I wear today?" Bert wonders.

Big Bird splashes in his morning bath with some friends.
"La! La! La! La! La!" he sings as he scrubs.

Rise and shine! Breakfast is served at Hooper's Store!

Don't forget to brush your fangs!

Be sure to comb your head—and face and elbows and knees!

It's a beautiful sunny day on Sesame Street!
All the monsters and birds and grouches have come out to play.

Rise and shine, little Elmo!